Bound to Dream

Bound to Dream

An Immigrant Story

Charles Ghigna

Charles Ghigna
Illustrated by Anna Forlati

Schiffer **Kids**®

4880 Lower Valley Road, Atglen, PA 19310

Designed by Jack Chappell
Cover design by Jack Chappell
Type set in Shift

ISBN (hardcover): 978-0-7643-6831-8
ISBN (e-book): 978-1-5073-0408-2
Printed in India

Published by Schiffer Kids
An imprint of Schiffer Publishing, Ltd.
4880 Lower Valley Road
Atglen, PA 19310
Phone: (610) 593-1777; Fax: (610) 593-2002
Email: info@schifferbooks.com
Web: www.schifferkids.com

For our complete selection of fine books on this and related subjects, please visit our website at www.schifferbooks.com. You may also write for a free catalog.

Schiffer Publishing's titles are available at special discounts for bulk purchases for sales promotions or premiums. Special editions, including personalized covers, corporate imprints, and excerpts, can be created in large quantities for special needs. For more information, contact the publisher.

In memory of my great-grandfather,
my grandfather, and my father

To my children, Chip and Julie;
my grandchildren, Charlotte and Christopher;
and all their children to come

And for Debra,
always

Carlo lived on a farm at the edge of a forest in Italy.
By day he milked cows and chopped wood.

At night after his chores, he read books by candlelight.

The warm smell of the leather book covers
and the faint scent of the forest rose from the pages.

The golden glow of candlelight filled his dreams
with people in faraway places.

One day when he was old enough,
Carlo sailed away on a steamship
across the ocean to New York City.

When he arrived at the port,
he joined a long line of people waiting to enter America.

Carlo walked the streets of the city for weeks looking for work.

It was a sad and lonely time for him.

He could not speak or read English very well,

and he missed his home and his family.

He felt lost in the big city

where no one knew his name.

One late afternoon just before sunset,
he stopped in front of a bookbinder shoppe
and looked in the window. He couldn't believe his eyes.

"So many beautiful books," he whispered to himself.

A kind old man came out of the shoppe and stood beside him.
"Are you looking for work?" asked the man. Carlo was silent.
The man looked closely at Carlo and noticed he was dressed
in the clothes of an immigrant. The man repeated his question in Italian:

Stai cercondo lavoro?

Carlo smiled up at the old man and said:

Sì.

Carlo soon learned the art of bookbinding. He learned how to tan leather
for the handsome book covers. He learned how to hand-stitch the pages together
to make the beautiful books he was learning to read in English.

Every night he sat up in his bed
looking at the books by the glow of the fire,
studying the words and the sentences,
practicing his English out loud to himself.

Word by word, page by page, he spent each night poring over his
books until the fire went out.

Carlo got up every morning and walked many blocks to the bookbinder shoppe.

He loved his books. He loved to make them and hold them in his hands, and he loved how he could smell the forest coming through the pages.

Carlo could almost feel the warmth of the cattle coming through the leather covers of his books.

Carlo was a quiet man, but when he spoke,
his words sounded like poetry.
When he grew older and had a family of his own,
he shared his story with them.

Carlo was my great-grandfather.
My father told me this story.

I never met my great-grandfather,
but I am grateful for the love he put in his books.

I am grateful for the love of books he put in me,
and I am grateful for the love of books in you.

Carlo (Charles) Vincent Ghigna was the author's great-grandfather.

He was born in Italy and immigrated to America in the 1800s.
He worked as a bookbinder in New York City.

Five generations of Carlo's descendants carry his name.

Charles Ghigna—Father Goose® was born in New York City and now lives in Homewood, Alabama, with his poet wife, Debra Holmes Ghigna. Their son, Charles (Chip) Vincent Ghigna V, is an artist. Charles is the author of more than 100 books, including *The Father Goose Treasury of Poetry*, *The Magic Box*, *A Poem Is a Firefly*, *Love Is Everything*, and *Fetch, Cat. Fetch!* He has written more than 5,000 poems for children and adults that have appeared in anthologies, newspapers, and magazines. He speaks at schools, conferences, libraries, and literary events throughout the US and overseas. For more information, visit his website at FatherGoose.com.

Anna Forlati was born in Padua, Italy. She received her degree in contemporary art and a degree in film history at the IUAV University in Venice. She has illustrated several books, and her work has appeared in many international exhibitions. She is a collaborator with the Onus Radio Magica Foundation. Her book *My Dad, My Rock* received a starred review from Kirkus Reviews.

WHAT IS BOOKBINDING?

Bookbinding is the art of cutting and sewing pages of a book together and attaching a sturdy book cover. Carlo used high-quality leathers for the book covers, and vellum papers for the pages. The leathers he used for the covers were from cows, pigs, sheep, and goats. Those leathers are the most supple and workable materials for book covers. The vellum Carlo used for the pages was made by stretching calfskin over a wooden frame and processing it into writing papers. Later, vellum pages were made by machines with cellulose fibers made from wood pulp and cotton. During Carlo's life, many fine books were made by hand. Today most books are made by machines.

More books by Charles Ghigna from Schiffer Kids®

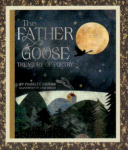

The Father Goose Treasury of Poetry: 101 Favorite Poems for Children
ILLUSTRATED BY SARA BREZZI
978-0-7643-6569-0

Fetch, Cat. Fetch!
ILLUSTRATED BY MICHELLE HAZELWOOD HYDE
978-0-7643-6460-0

A Poem Is a Firefly
ILLUSTRATED BY MICHELLE HAZELWOOD HYDE
978-0-7643-6108-1

Love Is Everything
ILLUSTRATED BY JACQUELINE EAST
978-0-7643-6223-1

The Magic Box: A Book of Opposites
ILLUSTRATED BY JACQUELINE EAST
978-0-7643-6778-6

Visit schifferkids.com